The Destitute Witch and Other Stories

Willi T. Florete

Ukiyoto Publishing

All global publishing rights are held by

Ukiyoto Publishing

Published in 2025

Content Copyright © Willi T. Florete

ISBN 9789370098046

All rights reserved.

No part of this publication may be reproduced, transmitted, or stored in a retrieval system, in any form by any means, electronic, mechanical, photocopying, recording or otherwise, without the prior permission of the publisher.

The moral rights of the author have been asserted.

This is a work of fiction. Names, characters, businesses, places, events, locales, and incidents are either the products of the author's imagination or used in a fictitious manner. Any resemblance to actual persons, living or dead, or actual events is purely coincidental.

This book is sold subject to the condition that it shall not by way of trade or otherwise, be lent, resold, hired out or otherwise circulated, without the publisher's prior consent, in any form of binding or cover other than that in which it is published.

www.ukiyoto.com

Dedication

This book is dedicated to God, who has blessed me with this opportunity. And of course, to my loving family, who are my ever-loyal readers and supporters.

Contents

The Destitute Witch	1
A Lucrative Gold-Mining Endeavor	5
Third Law of Motion	9
Dumpsite	11
The Sow in the Corner	17
The Destination of the Racing Heart	21
Mirror of Return	26
About the Author	*32*

The Destitute Witch

Mansano's heart slammed against his chest as he clambered up the stairs that led to his master's wide living room. He should have arrived here at six a.m. earlier; after all, the box of freshly baked *napoleones* that he had been tasked to buy from Quan every morning was what Doña Elly, his master, always ate at breakfast.

His arrival at Amaia, however, was delayed by the throng of people that had appeared in front of St. Catherine's Dormitory. According to what he had heard from a student (who was among the throng) earlier, the witch that the whole Eroreco had been attempting to capture was finally found in the said dormitory.

"Witch?" he had asked as his forehead creased. Truth was, he had wanted to scream until he ran out of air because of the early morning disturbance that had prevented him from returning to Doña Elly's condo. In spite of his frustration, however, he had kept his mouth shut. "That better be a true witch. Otherwise, traffic has clogged this part of the city for no good reason!"

"Ay, I'm not sure if it's a real witch, *manong*. I'm just here to watch the show." the student had replied, laughing heartily.

If only Mansano were not in a hurry to go back to his master's residence, he would have joined the student in his laughter.

***

"Into what hole have you been slithering, you kid?!" Doña Elly yelled as soon as Mansano was in the living room. "My children are already in Zaycoland so I have to make my way to Kabankalan *now*. Do you realize that I don't have time for breakfast, anymore? You really want me to starve during the trip, don't you?"

You do realize you can still eat in the van, don't you? Mansano thought. But aloud he replied, "I apologize, Ma'am. I couldn't get past La Salle Avenue right away because of traffic."

"Don't make excuses, *nonoy*. You're simply tardy. I'll just make deductions from your wage this month."

"Ma'am—"

"Give me the *napoleones*."

Mansano wanted to further explain what had happened, but he pursed his lips together because he knew too well that his master was not capable of understanding what other people went through.

"Here, Ma'am," he said, handing the *napoleones* to Doña Elly.

Doña Elly took her breakfast and replied, "Nelia texted me earlier. She said you will be cleaning her garden today, so you must go to her place this instant. Here's your fare for the jeep"—Doña Elly handed a twenty-peso bill to Mansano—"Off you go, then."

Mansano took the money with a nod. He went out of his master's condo, and upon reaching Amaia's entrance hall, he crossed paths with Miko, another servant of Doña Elly. The said boy was still seven years old, yet he was already working for the Doña.

"*'Nong*," Miko greeted, waving his hand. "How you doing?"

"Ay, not doing well, Mik. I got stuck in the traffic along La Salle Avenue earlier, so I was not able to return to the condo on time. Consequently, I got yelled at by Ma'am again."

"Sorry to hear that, *manong*. What caused the traffic, anyway?"

For a second, Mansano debated whether or not to tell Miko the real cause of the traffic earlier. After a moment of consideration, however, it dawned on him that there was nothing wrong with telling the truth to the kid.

"Well, someone told me earlier that a witch was found in St. Catherine's." Mansano confided, expecting the boy to burst out into laughter.

But Miko didn't laugh. He only looked at Mansano quizzically. "A witch?" he asked. "What is that?"

Now it was Mansano's turn to look at Miko quizzically. *I know that Miko's still a kid, but isn't it strange that he doesn't even know what a witch is?* he thought.

"Oh," Mansano started, "well, to put it simply, witches are creatures that eat humans. That's why they see the latter as mere objects that quench their hunger, further their pleasure, and maintain their comfort. It is for these reasons that humans like you and me should avoid them at all cost. Because witches are only good to their kind."

"Ay, witches are actually scary, aren't they?" Miko remarked.

"Indeed, Mik," Mansano replied, "Indeed."

***

"Traffic's still bad over here, huh?" Mansano thought to himself. The jeep he was riding in got enmeshed again in the hubbub that had been choking La Salle Avenue for about three hours now. Nothing much had changed since that baffling morning: onlookers still thronged in front of St. Catherine's; police officers, however, could now be seen in the premises of the dormitory.

When Mansano peered over his shoulder to look at the commotion, his eyes caught the sight of an old woman wearing a tattered and dingy dress. The said woman was flanked by two forty-year-old men whose condition was the same as hers. The jeep was not that far from the three, so Mansano managed to pick up what the old woman was saying: "Good thing you two are here. Good thing you two are here. If you hadn't been here, those people would have succeeded in taking me earlier. I'm not even a witch!"

No sooner had those words reached Mansano's ears than he realized that the pitiful woman was actually the alleged witch that the whole Eroreco had been trying to track and capture—which was preposterous and unjust, really, for it was obvious that the woman was nothing more than a human whose concerns mainly revolved around surviving each cruel day.

"Ay, may God bless you, *tiyay*," he thought to himself.

***

The sun was already casting everything in orange when Mansano arrived at his master's residence. Doña Nelia had given her a lot of tasks earlier, so his body was currently sore and aching. In spite of the pain and fatigue, however, he was still thankful that it was him whom the Doña had commissioned to clean the garden, because his efforts were once again rewarded with 400 pesos and a scrumptious lunch: *menudo*, rice, and caramel tarts from Merzci.

Mansano entered Doña Elly's condo with a sigh. He scanned the living room and, to his surprise, saw his master sitting on one of the sofas that occupied the space in the center of the *sala*. Doña Elly had told him last night that she and her children would be staying in Zaycoland for three days. That's why he found it strange that the Doña was currently in the condo. Curiosity tempted him to ask his master what had happened, but he kept his mouth shut because he knew that Doña Elly was only good to her family and relatives.

"My kids texted me earlier," the Doña suddenly said, "They said they wouldn't be able to make it to our excursion to Kabankalan."

It appears I don't need to ask anymore what's happened, Mansano thought. Aloud he said, "Ay, maybe soon you and your children will finally have the time to have that excursion, Ma'am."

"Perhaps," Doña Elly said, "perhaps."

"Well then, Ma'am," Mansano replied, "I'll start cleaning the house."

Mansano nodded and, before turning around, looked at his master, who continued to sit in silence. The Doña was accompanied by no one but herself.

Glossary:

nonoy - A Hiligaynon word used to address a boy who's younger than you

tiyay - A Hiligaynon word used to address old women

Doña - a title conferred on rich women

manong - a Hiligaynon word which means "big brother." The word is also used to address a guy older than you

'nong - clipped version of manong

A Lucrative Gold-Mining Endeavor

"Just drop me off by that yellow post up ahead, '*nong*." I yelled over the engine's noise as I rummaged in my wallet for a twenty-peso bill. With his face remaining completely blank, the driver sent the tricycle careening across Osmeña Street for a few seconds then made it skid to a stop in front of the yellow post.

"Thanks," I said as I handed my fare to the driver. I stepped out of the tricycle and walked over to the decrepit red gate that lay a few feet behind the yellow post. Heaving out a sigh, I opened the gate, which let out a loud metallic groan. I trudged through the now-open gate and, before closing it again, swept my gaze across the elementary school in front of *Tita*'s house, the palm trees lining the street, and the resplendent bougainvillea that wreathed one of the walls surrounding a nearby house. The sky was almost devoid of clouds, so everything was currently bathed in the sun's tawny, warm light.

The beautiful sight enchanted me, and if the circumstances were different, I would definitely spend the whole afternoon feasting my eyes on it. But I didn't leave the comforts of our home and come here to do that-although that would have been nice-but to accompany my grandmother who had been bedridden for eight months now. And so, taking off my sandals, I shuffled to the front door, opened it, and entered the living room. All of the windows in *Tita's* house opened either to another room or to a portion of the moss-covered wall (which was too close to her house) that encased her property. Which was why the inside of her house was perpetually dark and suffocating. Which was also why coming here was not something that I particularly looked forward to.

To be frank, I'd groaned silently earlier when *Lola* had called me on the phone and said that she was all alone at *Tita's* home. She didn't explicitly ask me to accompany her today, but I'd decided to spend the whole afternoon here anyway because doing the opposite would only make me feel like the most selfish person in the world. And so here I was, padding across *Tita's* living room, which, just like the other parts of her house, was perpetually dark and suffocating.

When I entered *Lola's* bedroom, she was lying on her bed with her eyes staring languidly at the ceiling. She looked more tired and fragile than last time, and immediately, deep gloom enveloped me. To catch her attention and to break the depressing silence, I knocked on her bedroom's door twice. With surprising swiftness, she turned her head in my direction.

"Hi, there," I chirped as soon as our eyes met. I walked to her bed and bent down to give her cheek a kiss.

"Oh, my *apo* is here?" she said weakly, her eyes widening in surprise.

"Of course," I replied, caressing her wrinkly hand. "So, how are you?"

Lola let out a tremulous sigh and said, "My thighs and my back always hurt-I can't even go to the bathroom next door to pee, so I always have a diaper on. I also find it hard to fall asleep at night. Last night, did you know? It took me until one in the morning to finally fall asleep."

I didn't know what to say in response to what she'd just said, so I asked her, "Have you been taking your medication regularly?"

"Well, of course. There's no chance I'll end up skipping it because your *tita* is hell-bent on making me take it on time."

To which I chuckled and replied, "That's a relief, then."

Lola shifted uncomfortably in her bed and stared at me with her rheumy eyes. "Oh, *totô*," she said, "what should I do? I don't think my situation will ever change. My body hurts every time I move-I'm practically stuck here in my bed. I-I don't want to be a burden to your *tita* and her family anymore."

Despite my will to appear brave and hopeful to *Lola*, sadness wreathed my face; and not so much because her confessions depressed me, but because I didn't know what to say to comfort her. The inability to comfort those who confided in me had always been one of the things that saddened and frustrated me.

I suddenly found it hard to breathe, so I sat on the edge of *Lola's* bed. "You've no reason to feel bad, '*La*,'" I began, "you're not being a burden to *Tita*. What child doesn't want to make sacrifices for their parents, anyway? Besides, haven't you done a lot for her and Mama? Had it not been for your and *Lolo's* hard work, they wouldn't have become professionals. Right now, Tita's simply repaying you for everything you've done for her."

"Oh, you think so?" *Lola* replied, her face relaxing a bit-to my relief.

"Yes."

Letting out a sigh, *Lola* asked, "Well, how's your mother?"

"She's busy as usual, but she's doing okay-slimmer, too."

"Ay, maybe she lost some weight because of stress."

"You sure? Maybe she's gone on a diet to make her and Papa's marriage spicier."

To my surprise, *Lola* let out a hearty laugh. I studied her face and saw that her eyes, which had looked weary just a few seconds ago, were now aglow. Her uneven white teeth even showed. I didn't know how my silly remark managed to extract such a loud laugh from her; it wasn't even that funny in my opinion. Regardless, relief filled me. Until now, I'd found it too laborious to breathe, and that was why I'd been anxious to leave and go home. Now, however, air entered and exited my nostrils with ease.

Lola placed her hand on mine and said in between chuckles, "Just tell your mother not to become so thin."

"I'll make sure to tell her that." I replied as I took in her wide smile, which emanated a golden glow.

Glossary:

LOLA - means "grandmother" in Hiligaynon

'LA - clipped form of Lola

'NONG - clipped form of Manong, a Hiligaynon word which is used to address one's elder brother or an older male stranger

TITA - means "aunt" in Hiligaynon

LOLO - means "grandfather" in Hiligaynon

TOTÔ - a Hiligaynon word used to address a younger boy

APO - means "grandchild" in Hiligaynon

Third Law of Motion

The tawny sunlight was streaming in through the wide window before me when the shopkeeper's bell jingled to announce a new diner. I set my cup of coffee on the saucer and turned to the restaurant's entrance. Through the doorway, a short, corpulent man passed. He wore a green t-shirt, a pair of blue jeans, and a deep frown.

The short, corpulent man weaved through the tables and stopped, to my surprise, before the group of men eating to my left. One of these men felt the short, corpulent man's presence and greeted the latter with a loud "Oy, *'mig*!" With a loud sigh, the short man pulled one of the chairs sitting around a nearby vacant table and settled beside his greeter. "Finally out of that cubicle," he said. To which his friends-at least I thought they were his friends-replied cheerfully, "Congrats."

"Got an earful from Sir Mal earlier," the short man continued, "he said my work was too disorganized. *Gwapo*, I don't get him. Not a single bit. How can my work be too disorganized when I spent over twenty hours to complete it?"

"Ay, ay," one of his friends said, "you know how that *gurang*'s head works. Because of his ripe age, he can't recognize a good work even when he sees one. Don't mind him!"

"But I bet he can't ever get mad at our Mr. *Pabibo*!" the short man's greeter from earlier said.

"Indeed!" the short man interjected in a voice that was now full of vigor. "Oh, I've had enough of that *bugalon*. He must think that just because he graduated from La Salle, he's already the smartest person in the company. Ha! Sir Mal praises him all the time not because his work is excellent, but because he is a Lasallian like him. I checked Mr. Lasalliano's work once, and it wasn't even close to being satisfactory."

"I couldn't agree more, *'mig*. You know what, why don't you order your food at the counter already? Forget about work. Let's just brim our stomachs with good food and good *panglibak* this afternoon. *Ayos*?"

"Sounds nice." The short man concurred as he stood up and walked toward the counter with, I noticed, a straighter back.

Glossary:

'mig - clipped version of "migo," which means "friend" in Hiligaynon

gwapo - means "handsome" in Hiligaynon. However, it is often used to express frustration

gurang - means "old person" in Hiligaynon

pabibo - a Hiligaynon word used to refer to people who tend to show off

bugalon - means "arrogant" in Hiligaynon

panglibak - means "gossiping" or "backstabbing" in Hiligaynon

ayos - means "okay" in Hiligaynon

Dumpsite

If he were not so frustrated at the heap of garbage currently sitting in his backyard, Mr. Malawa would be enjoying this copacetic morning right now. If only he'd chosen to stop griping, then by now he would be enjoying the blazing sun rising above the treetops and the glinting dews that had clung to the bougainvilleas that he himself had been tending to. But no-as of the moment, his eyes were nothing but loyal beholders of this mountain of wastes currently defiling his morning.

"*Bwisit*!" he exclaimed as he glared at the slimy bags of garbage. "Why are these still here?"

Upon hearing his father's scream of infuriation, Jess, who was preparing a cup of coffee, went out of the kitchen and strode over to the old man's side. "Is something wrong that you are screaming like this?" he asked.

"Why are these still here?" Mr. Malawa repeated, pointing tremulously at the engenderers of his wrath. "Shouldn't have your cousin brought them outside at 6 a.m. earlier? The garbage truck passes by our house around that time, after all. *Tê*? Now that the *basureros* have already left our *purok*, what are we going to do with these?" At which Mr. Malawa gestured at the bags of garbage with more vehemence.

"Well-"

"That sloth," Mr. Malawa said, not caring to let his son finish, "Isn't it his duty to bring the garbage out every morning? Call him this very instant. That brat needs an earful."

"Oh, Papa. Let this shortcoming of your nephew's slide just this once. Wasn't he the one who finished all of Mikka's projects last night so that the two of you could make an excursion to the Lagoon? And, for goodness' sake, he's just a thirteen-year-old kid. He's bound to make mistakes every once in a while, right?"

"Shut that mouth of yours already, Jess. Besides, if that cousin of yours knew that he wouldn't be able to wake up early the next day-well, thanks to the sacrifice that he made for your sister-then why didn't he bring the garbage out before he slept last night? That would have been the smart thing to do. Anyone who'd been in their right mind would have done that!"

"Pa, you know as much as I do that that is inadvisable. After all, leaving the garbage outside for too long will just give the stray dogs a chance to scatter them all over the street."

"Whatever! Just call Mark. *Hurry*."

Seeing that arguing with his father would bear no fruit, Jess acquiesced and did as he was told. Deep inside, he didn't want Mark to be berated. He was unable to fulfill his task today, yes, but that failure of his was not a result of an irresponsible behavior, but of a selfless deed. "Hadn't Papa tasked Mark to complete Mikka's school work last night, he would've had the energy to wake up early today and bring the garbage out." Jess thought to himself.

Jess was against what his father was about to do, but he knew that in the end, only the latter's wishes would prevail. Which was why, as much as it revolted him, he woke Mark up and brought him to the old man's side. And though he knew that his presence wouldn't prevent his father from reprimanding Mark, he still chose to stay beside the boy-if only to accompany him in the scary experience that he was about to go through.

"Today you only had one job," Mr. Malawa said malignantly without looking away from the heap of garbage, "and you didn't even manage to fulfill it."

"I apologize, *Tito*. I was-" Mark began.

"Shut up! I don't want to hear your excuses." At which Mark's head bowed down. "You ungrateful kid. Do you have any idea how much I spend for you every month? Oh"-Mr. Malawa massaged his temples- "I don't even want to think about it."

"I-I'll do better next time, Tito." Mark offered querulously.

"You-know your place, okay? If I didn't take you in, you would be sleeping on the streets right now. Mark my words, *totô*-unless you turn your back on this indolence of yours, you won't ever succeed in the future, let alone stand on your own feet. So do yourself a favor and work hard like a real man, got it?"

"Yes, *Tito*. I'll keep those words in mind."

"You'd better!" Mr. Malawa scoffed. "The least thing you can do to repay everything that I've done for you is fulfill your duties in this house. Now, go and prepare breakfast. Go. Go." Mr. Malawa made a shooing motion with his hand. Apparently he was anxious to rid his sight of his nephew's face.

"But what about the garbage, *Tito*? Shouldn't I take them-"

"Forget about them! Why bother to worry about them now when you couldn't even take care of them earlier? Now, I beg you, get out of my sight before I smack you for real."

With his hands hanging limply at his sides, Mark made his way back inside the kitchen. The weak slapping sound that his slippers made on the floor broke not only the thick silence that had permeated the air, but also Jess' heart, which pounded violently with rage.

"Jess," Mr. Malawa said to his son as soon as Mark was out of earshot, "prepare the *traysikol* because you will be loading these smelly things in it. Since the *basureros*-"

"Was it really necessary to castigate Mark like that, Papa? I mean, he only failed to bring the garbage out today because he had stayed up late last night to finish Mikka's school works. Isn't it unfair for him, Papa? Oh, I can only imagine how deflated he is right now." Jess said weakly.

"This kid," Mr. Malawa sighed exasperatedly, "haven't we talked about this already? What's the matter with you, really? Isn't it only right to rebuke and discipline those who have committed an error? It's common sense, Jess. Besides, words are just words; I didn't even hit him, did I? That cousin of yours will recover in no time. You'll see. He's now big enough to handle a little rebuke."

"But-"

"Enough of this talk already. Just go and load these"—he motioned to the heap of garbage—"in the *traysikol*. And once you're done loading them, go to that vacant lot behind Terisa's and dump them there. Still remember Terisa's, right? The eatery we always pass by every time we pass through Lopez Jaena Street?"

"Yes, of course. But-"

"Good. Dump the garbage in the vacant lot behind it."

"W-Wait, are we even allowed to do that? Won't that be damage of property or something?"

"Hey, that lot is practically a home to ghosts. It's not even up for sale. Just do as I say, got it? It's not like I'm asking you to vandalize someone else's property."

Eight minutes later, Jess found himself standing in front of the vacant lot that his father had told him to go to. It was a twelve-by-fifteen-meter-wide piece of land immured by the jagged remains of the brick walls that must have stood prominently back in the days of past. Through the gaps in the said lot's concrete surface, resplendent fever roots grew. Old mahogany trees, whose healthy leaves were swaying in the soft breeze and glinting in the morning sun, also ran along its northern edge, which was a long and narrow strip of earth.

"This place is surprisingly beautiful," Jess thought to himself as memories from his childhood flashed in his mind. He particularly remembered that time when he was brought by his parents to Molo, Iloilo City for the first time. He was still fourteen back then, and his mother hadn't been snatched by breast cancer yet. The three of them had had a lovely time there. They'd tried every restaurant they could find on Benigno Aquino Ave., they'd watched *Heneral Luna* at the cinema, and, just to simply pass the time, they'd promenaded along the major avenues of the city, feasting their eyes on the tall, bright buildings that had stood almost everywhere and on the spacious parks that had occasionally popped into view.

To Jess, those days were the best moments of his life, and he knew full well that none of the days in the future would ever be able to equal them. He also knew, with grim certainty, that for now (and for the rest of his life, for that matter), he had to make do with days riddled with dullness, bitterness, and bereftness.

"Well, no time for sentimentality right now." Jess muttered under his breath as he rolled up the cuffs of his sweater. Terisa's would open any moment now. If the owners of the eatery found him dumping garbage in the lot that was right behind their establishment, things would definitely take an awkward turn. And so, he began his work. One by one, he heaved the bags of garbage out of the *traysikol* and propped each of them up against one of the mahogany trees. It had been a while since the last time he'd exerted this much physical effort, so just a few minutes into the task, his arms began to ache.

He managed to persist through the pain, though. And before he knew it, he was already regarding the finished work of his still-trembling hands. The bags of garbage were now neatly clumped around the mahogany tree, and in the glare of the ever-rising sun, they seemed like giant dog ticks. What an awful sight to behold, Jess thought.

So as not to waste any more time, he turned around and made his way back to the *tarysikol*. He didn't have much energy left, so his limbs felt like noodles. With all the strength that he could muster, he swung his leg over the motorcycle and inserted the key in the ignition; before turning it, however, he gave the vacant lot a final look. To his surprise- and dismay-the ethereal glamor that it had possessed earlier was not present anymore.

Earlier he had thought that even if he put the bags of garbage in the vacant lot, the latter's pristine beauty would still remain intact because the wastes weren't even that plenty. The dingy state that it was now in, however, told him that his initial thoughts had been wrong.

Wearily, Jess swept his gaze across the now-defiled plot of land that lay before him. It had looked like a haven earlier when he hadn't begun working yet. But now all it resembled was a desolate and dingy ruin that evoked regrets, sorrows, and unrealized dreams.

Glossary:

bwisit - An expression of frustration in Hiligaynon

tê - a Hiligaynon word which means "so"

basurero - Means "garbage collectors" in Hiligaynon

tito - Means "uncle" in Hiligaynon
totô - A Hiligaynon term used to address a boy
traysikol - The Hiligaynon spelling for "tricycle"

The Sow in the Corner

If I'd had a say in this foolishness, I would have left the table long before Mother could set any of the chinaware. Heck—I would have even gone to Kabankalan to drink Iced Americano at Spanishtown. For who in their right mind would stay at this gathering? Only a lunatic would sit silently on their hard-backed chair and watch the adults force a smile and talk as if nothing was amiss.

I clenched my hands into fists and groaned inwardly. I wanted to stand up and run out of the house, but since I was just a mere lad who was not allowed to decide for himself, I continued sitting tight and putting up with this cringe-worthy show that everyone was performing.

"Shall we say grace now?" Mother said demurely, sweeping her gaze across the faces around the table.

Tita Riya, my father's elder sister, replied, "Sure." At which everyone uttered in perfect unison the mealtime prayer "Bless Us, O Lord."

"Let's dig in, then," Father said as soon as the prayer was over. He snatched the bowl of rice and dumped a lavish pile of the steaming white grain on Rosie's plate. The sight of it made my heart pump faster. If only I could roll my eyes and say, "Aw, what a sweet father," my anger would certainly be appeased. But I couldn't. So I made do with cursing him in my mind.

"You've gotten scrawny, haven't you?" my aunt's husband said to me as he pinched my shoulder. "You should eat more, boy. Otherwise, you'll be left with nothing but bones."

"Will do, *Tito*," I replied, surreptitiously watching Father ladling menudo on top of Rosie's rice.

"Have you already decided where to study for college, Rosie?" Mother asked as she put rice on her plate.

For a second, Rosie looked at Mother sheepishly. And then, "I . . . thought it would be good to study at TUP."

"She's decided to take up Engineering!" Father exclaimed with pride. "Can you believe that? She's paving her very own road."

"I daresay she's as intelligent as you, Ton-ton," *Tita* Riya remarked.

Father chuckled and seconded, "She is smart, all right."

The compliment made Rosie flush. "I'm just hoping for the best," she said.

"Don't worry. Your Mama Nina and I will be supporting you."

No sooner had those words left Father's mouth than a wave of anger surged through me. "How dare you!" I uttered under my breath. I looked at Mother just in time to see a muscle in her jaw twitch. I tried calming my racing heart down but to no avail. My effort to still myself had only intensified my already raging rage.

"Right, Ma?" Father said to Mother, grinning widely.

Mother took a deep breath and replied, "Of course."

And at that moment, I finally snapped. Before I could stop myself, I pushed my chair back from the table and stood up. Everyone stopped speaking and turned to me.

"I-I'm sorry," I started, "but may I be excused? I need to go to the bathroom."

"Sure, sure," Father said, "but go back here right away, okay? We still have so many things to talk about."

I let out a grunt in response.

***

Truth was, I didn't go to the bathroom; right after exiting the kitchen, I went straight to the pigpen, which lay about eight meters south of the house. I couldn't handle staying near Father anymore, so I'd decided to flee the "family gathering." This relief, however, would only be brief, for it was only a matter of time before Father or someone else from the table went out of the house and asked me to return to our lunch. "Better than no respite at all." I muttered under my breath.

I swept my gaze across the surprisingly clean pigpen that housed one boar, two sows, and over a dozen piglets, which were all sucking frenetically on the teats of the weak-looking sow lying down in a far corner.

"Your father's treasures," a voice behind me suddenly said, making me jump.

I whirled around and saw *Tita* Riya's husband.

"Sorry—didn't mean to startle you," he continued, chuckling. He walked past me and stood before the pigpen. "He really treasures these pigs, your father. He always talks about them whenever we're having a drink. So it's not a surprise that they've grown on me. Look"—he pointed to the sow standing beside the boar—"that gal was purchased by your father and me about four months ago to 'spice things up.' Well, things did spice up, all right. But see, our newcomer here is incapable of producing milk, so she can't feed her own young. Your father had initially planned to buy milk replacers, but when he found out how much they cost, he abandoned the idea altogether.

"Oh, I can still remember how frustrated and defeated his face looked at that time. Fortunately for him, though, I was there to give him the solution to his problem: make mating partner number one nurse the farrows of mating partner number two."

Tita Riya's husband guffawed and leaned his hands against one of the pigpen's low walls. "You should have seen how your father's face lit up after hearing my wise advice. He looked like a boy who received his toy gun for the first time! Oh"—he sighed and crossed his arms over his chest—"so, until your father can afford to buy milk replacers, mating partner number one has to nurse not just her children, but also the children of her fellow sow."

I didn't know why he was telling me all this, nor did I know what to say in response. So I remained silent and stayed put even though every fiber of my being was telling me to walk away and look for another solitary place.

"Let's go back to our lunch now, shall we?" he said, turning to me.

"You go on ahead, *Tito*. I'll go back to the kitchen in a minute." I replied, hoping he'd realize I needed some time with myself.

"Ay, *hindi*. Told you: you should eat more if you don't want to be left with nothing but bones."

I'd rather starve than eat with you lot, I thought. Aloud I said: "Okay."

Glossary:

Tita - means "aunt" in Hiligaynon

Tito - means "uncle" in Hiligaynon

hindi - means "no" in Hiligaynon

The Destination of the Racing Heart

"Are you sure about your decision? I mean, have you carefully thought it over?" Jessie asks Merny, her forehead creasing in concern. The question disappoints Merny; after all, she told Jessie about her decision in the hope that the latter would approve of it-which would in turn give her peace of mind. Approval, however, is not what she has received, and immediately she regrets telling her *manang* that she's finally decided to be in a relationship with Sam.

"Yes, '*nang*," Merny replies, doing her best to sound certain and firm. "This may sound foolish, but I know that my decision is right."

Jessie's brows rise, and for a second doubt and worry wreath her face. If there is one thing that she's sure of, it's that Merny does not yet understand what being in a relationship means and entails. Taking a deep breath, she says to Merny, "Mern, you know I care about you, right? You're like a sister to me, so I don't want you to fall into trouble by making big decisions like this so rashly. So please don't take offense at my questions.

"You see, at your young age, you still don't understand what love is. Perhaps you are now sick of this sort of admonition because you have heard it plenty of times already, but what I've just told you is true, Mern. Look at me-I'm already twenty-five and yet I'm still single! And that's because I know that entering a relationship with someone is a serious matter and that rushing into it without careful thought is destructive. So please answer me honestly: have you carefully thought your decision over?"

Merny wants so badly to give a reply, but no string of words can form in her mind, so she bows her head down and remains quiet instead, hoping that by doing so she can put a stop to her *manang's* inquisition. Her silence, however, only confirms Jessie's suspicion. In a crude attempt to convince her *manang*, Merny says, "Yes, *manang*. Believe me, I have!"

Seeing that Merny does not have any intention of telling her the truth, Jessie relents. "Well, then," she says. "I wish your relationship with Sam the best."

Merny knows that despite her calm voice, Jessie is frustrated and dismayed. But that doesn't concern or bother her, because she believes that she is in good hands, which were Sam's.

***

Merny saw Sam for the first time when she was being interviewed by *The Spectacles*' (the University of Bacolod's student publication) section editors in the empty room on Cafe Bob's second floor. A couple of weeks prior to this interview, she had sent an application letter to the publication's office to inform its editorial board of her desire "to become one of the fabled publication's feature writers." She had never really expected to pass the initial screening-she had merely submitted the application letter to see if *The Spectacles* would ever deem her a good enough student journalist.

Two days after she'd made that submission, however, she received an email from the publication that said she was one of the applicants whom they would interview in about two to three weeks. She couldn't believe the news that reached her. In fact, it wasn't until *The Spectacles* sent her a second email-this time, to inform her of the date and venue of the interview-that its reality finally sank into her.

During the interview, the first question came from Andrea Mantiles, the publication's managing editor. "How do you handle writer's block?" she asked Merny, smiling sweetly.

The question did not jar Merny-it was one of the questions for which she had made an answer beforehand. Plucking the memorized answer from her memory, she replied with relative confidence, "I handle it by reviewing the outline I've constructed. It helps me reacquaint myself with the structure and the theme of the piece I'm writing."

If Andrea was satisfied with Merny's answer, she did not show it. She simply continued smiling and said, "Your turn, Ley." She was referring to Leo Balboa, the publication's copy editor. Deftly crossing his legs, Leo asked Merny rather condescendingly, "What makes you think you're cut out for the publication?"

This time, the question shook whatever meager confidence Merny had. She hadn't prepared for it in advance, so she wasn't sure what kind of answer would reach the copy editor's standards, which she was sure were lofty. Her diffidence became even worse when, just a few seconds after he asked his first question, Leo raised another inquest which, to her, felt like an attack on her very worth: "What makes you think you deserve to be accepted into *The Spectacles*?"

Before Merny knew it, her heart had begun racing. She tried calming down by telling herself that a position at the publication was not even that important so she shouldn't take the interview seriously. Her strategy, however, did not prove to be effective. There was just something about Leo's piercing stare and stentorian tone that made her feel anxious.

She stared down at the tileless floor and would have burst into tears hadn't an equally stentorian but kind voice broken the silence. "Oh, come on, Ley," it said, "there's no need to be so harsh. We all come from humble positions, don't we?"

Leo took his eyes from Merny and turned them to the source of the voice. "Is there something wrong with asking a valid question, Sam?" he said. "Besides, I was merely checking her capability to handle pressure, and based on the results, Sammy, hers is not that good."

To Leo's outburst, Sam only responded with a smile. He stood from his chair and sauntered over to Leo's side. He bent down and, with a wider smile flashing on his face, whispered something into Leo's ear. Merny didn't know what he had surreptitiously told Leo, but it certainly succeeded in making the condescending lad to relent. Even the piercing stare that he had been wearing earlier vanished. Merny looked at Sam, her rescuer, and hoped that she could thank him aloud for putting Leo in his place. The presence of the other section editors, however, prevented her from uttering a word of gratitude. So she flashed the sincerest smile she could exhibit instead and hoped that it was not lost on Sam.

From that point on the interview went smoothly, and Merny had never been so thankful to someone in her life. When the whole thing was over, she walked over to Sam-who, at that time, was standing in a far corner staring intently at his phone-and, braving through her shyness and hesitations, told him she was thankful for his defending her from Leo earlier. Sam looked her in the eye and smiled, which caused her heart to race uncontrollably.

"In the end," Sam replied, "people like him are the real losers. They put others down not because they believe they're superior to them, but because deep down they are insecure."

"That-" Merny gathered her thoughts, "*that* is so true."

Sam found her vehement concurrence adorable and chuckled. "Here's a tip: forget what happened earlier and just relax," he said. "You did well in the interview-I've a strong feeling you'll be one of our new members. Why don't we have coffee downstairs while the section eds are still finalizing their decision?"

The offer surprised Merny, and for a moment she struggled to collect herself. She just couldn't believe that Sam, who was no less than an impressive guy, had asked her to drink coffee with him. "Sure, '*nong*. As long as it's your treat." she said when she had finally composed herself.

To which Sam replied with another chuckle, "Well, don't *manongs* always do that for their *manghods*?"

Since this brief encounter, the two had became close. And in the days that followed Merny's acceptance into *The Spectacles* as a magazine writer, Sam consistently stayed by her side and conversed with her. It is no surprise, really, that just after a month, the two reached a point where they had mutual feelings for each other.

When two months had passed since Merny got accepted into the publication, Sam invited her to go to the Negros Museum to see the paintings of Mathia Aming, which were being exhibited there at that time. "I just thought it would be good to spend some time with you at the museum," Sam told her, smiling. "I mean, don't lovers always do that in movies?" At which Merny stared at Sam with wide eyes and a racing heart. What Sam had just said was as good as a confession of his feelings for her, and she couldn't believe that he'd managed to make that profession without any hint of nervousness or hesitation.

Merny was not sure what to think or say-heck, she couldn't even wrap her head around Sam's confession yet-but of this she was certain: she was ecstatic about being in a relationship with him. She could barely wait to experience what was in store for them as lovers.

When they got to the Negros Museum, Merny couldn't focus on the paintings that were on display before them. No-it's more accurate to say that she couldn't care less about them, because at that moment, all her eyes sought was Sam's face. *Sam*, she thought, *how did I end up with a great guy like you?*

"Thank you so much for your patronage, sir," a raspy voice suddenly said, snatching Merny from her reverie. She turned to where the voice came from and saw a man in a dark green polo shirt and white slacks. The said man, who seemed to be in his early thirties, was talking to Sam, who in turn was gesturing at a particular painting.

"Can I be honest with you? I'm actually surprised that a young lad such as yourself has decided to purchase one of Miss Aming's works," the man continued, "not so much because youths don't usually have the financial capacity to buy the works of art featured at this museum, but because in most cases only adults can understand and appreciate our Miss Aming's paintings."

"Can I also be honest with you?" Sam replied, leaning closer to the man. "I've decided to acquire the painting not because I understand it, but because I find it pleasing to the eyes."

The man slightly drew his head back and stared at Sam incredulously, as if what the latter had said was the most foolish thing in the world. "But if you don't know what it means, why buy it?" he asked. "You do realize that if you don't understand the essence of this painting you're about to possess, it will be almost impossible for you to truly value and appreciate it, right?"

"Let's not be too critical now, shall we, Sir? Weren't we put here on this good earth to simply enjoy ourselves? Who said we should live life so critically?"

"Fair enough. After all, to please people is one of the purposes of art."

"Precisely. Now, could you please process my purchase already? My girlfriend and I still have places to explore."

Sam wrapped his arm around Merny's shoulders and gave her a smile, which, as usual, caused her heart to race uncontrollably.

Mirror of Return

Leaning back in his monoblock chair, Sir Dino paused for a moment in typing on his laptop to regard what he had accomplished so far. *Not bad. I've made quite a lot of progress today,* he thought. Their research defense would be on Saturday this week; today was Tuesday. It was true that he had already completed many parts of their research paper, but he was worried nonetheless because they hadn't conducted their study yet.

If they wanted to complete their study in time for the defense, they must finish the distribution of the survey questionnaires before Thursday. If it were up to him, he would, right this moment, give their questionnaires to the senior high school students (their chosen respondents) of the school he was teaching at. Their co-researcher, however, was still in the process of getting their letter of request to conduct a study signed by their course instructor at CPSU Main in Barangay Camingawan, which was an almost-two-hour ride from Hinigaran.

Actually, yesterday, he had given their initial letter of request to conduct a study to Ma'am Samantha, the principal of their school. But when Ma'am Samantha had seen that it hadn't been signed by their course instructor yet, she had told him that she wouldn't allow him and his co-researchers to conduct the study until their course instructor's signature could be seen on the said letter. Truth was, Sir Dino had gotten a little upset. He had also wondered why Ma'am Samantha didn't allow him to proceed with the distribution of their survey questionnaires because when he had consulted his elder brother (who was teaching at the same school as him) two days ago, the latter had told him that in the past, he had still managed to get Ma'am Samantha's permission even if the letter he had presented to her did not contain their course instructor's signature.

"What has changed now, then?" he uttered under his breath, seething.

He was not sure if their co-researcher would succeed in getting their letter signed by their course instructor today. Perhaps something untoward would happen and then the completion of their study would be delayed further. Or maybe by the time he gave Ma'am Samantha their signed letter of request, she would still choose to forbid them to conduct their study. If either of these bleak possibilities happened, what should they do? Suddenly, Sir Dino's chest tightened. He closed the Word document of their research paper and sighed shakily. He shut his eyes and opened his mouth to pray, but before a word could escape his lips, what he'd done last night flashed in his mind.

He shouldn't have gone to that website. He shouldn't have looked at such a vile thing. He shouldn't have indulged in immorality even if the temptation at that time was irresistible. For the second time that morning, his chest tightened. He blew air out of his mouth so he could breathe. He suddenly remembered that he actually had a class at 8:05 a.m. He threw a glance at his wristwatch and saw that it was now 8:02. He hastily wrapped his things up: he shut his laptop and grabbed his phone from the table. Then, with his laptop in his left hand and his phone in the other, he set off to the classroom of his first class, which was two rooms to the right of their office.

On entering the classroom, he was accosted by the noise of his grade eight students. He swept his gaze across the room and saw that almost all of his students were either standing or roaming about even if he had already entered. A part of him was glad that his students were so comfortable around him that they were not afraid to be at ease in his presence, but there was also a big part of him that felt dismayed and insulted because his students were not giving him the respect that they readily gave to their strict teachers; which was tragic, because if there was someone who truly deserved their respect, it would be him, who had always been patient with and considerate of them.

Thing was, Sir Dino didn't want to be strict with his students because he didn't want them to feel afraid every time he entered the classroom. But sometimes he couldn't help but wonder whether his being a friendly and "chill" teacher was still right.

He set his things on the teacher's table and, in a loud voice, told his students to take their seats and settle down. The students did sit down, but Sir Dino knew too well that it was only a matter of time before they became noisy again.

"So, how are you all?" he asked the class.

"Just fine, Sir."

"Tired, Sir."

"So far, still alive, Sir."

Sir Dino started checking the attendance and, as he had expected, his students became noisy again. He, however, did not tell them off yet; the discussion hadn't started yet, after all. But as soon as he was done checking the attendance, he once again told his students to settle down and started the discussion. Actually, they were a bit behind on their lessons because of the many activities that their school had held last week. Sir Dino wanted so much to start their discussion today with a motivational activity, but if he were to do that, chances were they would not be able to finish discussing all of their topics for this quarter.

"Okay, listen now," he said in Hiligaynon, although their mode of instruction in ESP was supposed to be Tagalog. "Before we proceed to our next lesson, can someone from the class tell me what we discussed last week?"

Danica, one of his most studious students, promptly raised her hand at his question. Sir Dino appreciated this child not only because she was smart, but also because he could see that she was sincerely interested in their lessons. If all of his grade eight students were like her, then certainly he wouldn't get tired from reprimanding misbehaving students ever again.

"We learned about the kinds of friendship, Sir." the child replied.

"Very good." Sir Dino was going to discuss their new lesson, but before he could do so, Arvin, easily the unruliest student in the class, stood up and scampered to his friend, Mia, who sat in the other column of chairs. He then started talking to her loudly. Sir Dino was infuriated because Arvin acted as if he was not inside the classroom. What he was doing right now was nothing short of insulting. His being noisy and unruly disrupted the discussion. What was worse, his classmates saw what he was doing as a warrant for talking loudly with their seatmates as well. And before Sir Dino knew it, the whole room was once again filled with clamor.

Sir Dino's blood boiled. He knew he shouldn't be angry, but he couldn't stop his anger from simmering within him. He'd had enough of life. Besides, hadn't he been putting up with these misbehaving kids for too long already? It was now time to remind them who was truly in charge inside the classroom.

Seething, Sir Dino glared at Arvin and said to him, "What is your problem? Are you that hungry for attention? Return to your seat, will you? You're behaving like a kid whose brain hasn't fully developed yet. Keep acting like that and I will have you confined to a mental hospital."

The last remark sent the whole class laughing. Those who were near Arvin sneered at him and called him *buang-buang*—crazy. In no time, shame filled the child. He bowed his head so his classmates wouldn't be able to look him in the eye. He shuffled to his armchair and flopped on it. That he was able to put Arvin in his place should have satisfied Sir Dino, but satisfaction was not what filled him at this moment, but guilt. He knew that what he did was wrong. He shouldn't have spoken to the child like that. He should have corrected him gently instead. His words just now didn't glorify God at all.

The guilt remained with him until the class ended. Actually, it didn't leave him even when he had already set foot in their office. He sat at his desk and set up his laptop so he could resume working on their thesis. Sir Dino wanted to prepare PowerPoint presentations for their lessons and to make summative tests, but their thesis was more urgent right now. If he didn't prioritize it, for sure they would have no paper to submit this Saturday.

Once again, he opened the Word file of their thesis. He set his fingers on the keyboard of his laptop, but before he could start typing, Arvin's downcast face from earlier flashed in his mind. Sir Dino realized that Arvin was still a child who was yet to learn many things, so the boy's misbehavior earlier was not caused by his desire to irritate him, but by the fact that he did not yet understand what he was doing. In other words, he couldn't help but behave that way. Sir Dino remembered that he himself, when he was still a kid, was not aware at all of how his actions would affect other people.

What have I done? Sir Dino thought as, finally, he began working on their thesis.

***

Sir, our letter of request is not yet signed up to now because Doc Gina was not at CPSU anymore when I arrived there yesterday.

Sir Dino wished that the words before him were not true, but no matter how many times he read the chat of his co-researcher, the news that reached him did not change. And even if he didn't want to, he began to tremble and feel cold. He bit one of his fingernails to calm himself down.

Actually, he had gone to school early so that once he received the scanned copy of their signed letter of request, he could print it right away and bring it to their principal. But what greeted him this morning was nothing but bad news.

Out of habit, Sir Dino began to pray to raise his concern to God. And no sooner had he done so than his anxiety subsided. The weight that had been pressing on his heart since the moment he woke up gradually lifted. This peace, however, did not last long, because without warning, he suddenly remembered what he'd done two nights ago.

His heart felt heavy again. He wanted so badly to remain in the Lord's presence, but he couldn't shake off the feeling that he was not worthy of being near to God. He was too dirty to approach even the edge of His glory.

And so, when the bell rang, he went to his first class with a troubled heart. He set his laptop and other things on the teacher's desk without his usual liveliness. He straightened up his back to start the class, only to be startled by his student Arvin, who, unbeknownst to him, had scampered beside him. That Arvin was currently by his side surprised him. He hadn't thought the boy would approach him today because it was only yesterday that he had reprimanded him.

But here Arvin was, standing at his side without a single hint of fear or hesitation. The boy surprised Sir Arvin even more by speaking to him in a jovial voice, "You've brought a lot of papers, Sir, *'no?* What are they?"

"Your answer sheets from our last summative test." Sir Dino replied, looking at Arvin incredulously.

"Oh, is that so, Sir? Do you want me to return them to my classmates?"

Sir Dino smiled. He liked how relaxed and comfortable Arvin around him was. Actually, he was relieved that the boy was now talking to him this way, because it meant that the harsh words that he had flung at him yesterday did not affect him that terribly. If up to this moment Arvin was still downcast or keeping his distance from him, Sir Dino's guilt, which hadn't relented since yesterday, would definitely intensify.

"Go on, then," Sir Dino replied, "give them back to your classmates."

At which Arvin took the bundle of one-half lengthwise intermediate papers and immediately began distributing them to their owners. As Sir Dino looked at the boy, he realized something. No—it is more accurate to say that he remembered something, and that was a truth that he had long learned; a truth that he had heard plenty of times during their church services at Victory Kabankalan; a truth that, all this time, he had been doubting.

I should learn from this boy, Father, Sir Dino prayed, chuckling. *Are you not more compassionate and forgiving than me?*

For the first time in two days, a smile blossomed on Sir Dino's face. He breathed in the humid but refreshing air and stared out of the classroom's doorway. His eyes were met by the view of the school's untended but beautiful field. The brilliant morning sunlight had bathed the blanket of scraggly grass in gold, and the sight filled Sir Dino with peace and joy that he thought he would never feel again.

He sighed, but this time, out of relief. Later, he, too, would enter the presence of the One he had wronged. Not with fear, but with confidence.

About the Author

Willi T. Florete

Willi T. Florete is an aspiring fictionist and poet who currently resides in Hinigaran, Negros Occidental. In 2022, he graduated Cum Laude from the University of St. La Salle - Bacolod with a Bachelor's Degree in Secondary Education Major in English. In 2024, his poem The Slaughter was published in Hut;k Bacolod's (a Bacolod-based poetry folio) second volume Flutter. He actively writes short stories and poems during his free time. At present, he is a senior high school teacher at Hinigaran National High School.

www.ingramcontent.com/pod-product-compliance
Lightning Source LLC
LaVergne TN
LVHW041642070526
838199LV00053B/3513